I AM a Superhero

Jeannette Paxia
Author

Barbara Alvarado
Illustrator

Balboa Press
A Division of Hay House
1663 Liberty Drive
Bloomington, IN 47403
www.balboapress.com
844-682-1282

Interior Image Credit: Barbara Alvarado

ISBN: 978-1-9822-5752-1 (sc)
ISBN: 978-1-9822-5753-8 (e)

Library of Congress Control Number: 2020921316

Balboa Press rev. date: 11/05/2020

BALBOA.PRESS
A DIVISION OF HAY HOUSE

Dedication

Jeannette — This book is dedicated to Brian and my friends and family who have always supported me. To Barbara, my friend and illustrator, thank you for bringing my words to life. I am so proud of all you have done to provide a beautiful space for people to express their creativity, DragonFly Art For Life is one of my favorite places to go. Miriam Laundry, author of several children's books, including the recent book The Big Bad Bully. Her book I CAN Believe in Myself, set a Guinness World Record™ in 2014. Thank you for the inspiration to create a shorter version of my book You ARE a Superhero. To Founder of the Jesse Lewis, Choose Love Foundation, Scarlett Lewis is such an inspiration to me, showing how one can react with love in response to tragedy. I am in awe of what she has created, visit the foundation site https://chooselovemovement.org/.

To my children and stepchildren continue to use your talents to help the world. My most important job is to be your mom, to show you how to live life to the fullest in accordance with your purpose.

Barbara — This book is dedicated to my girls, Elizabeth and Danielle, thank you for always believing in me. To my parents who have supported my dreams. To Jeannette, my friend, who gave me this opportunity to create and to God for His love and blessings throughout my life.

We would also like to thank Mrs. Gaitan's class from Aspire Summit Charter Academy and Sonoma Elementary school in Modesto, California, for having Jeannette as a guest speaker. Your input on changes that should be made to the book, helped us in making the book better. We appreciate your ideas and suggestions.

In the world of my dreams, I can jump so high

that I can fly through the sky,

like a bird,

like a plane.

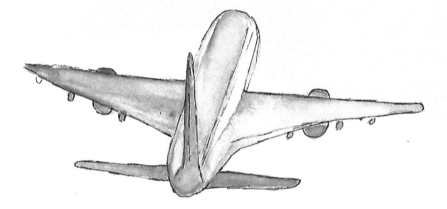

But as my mom wakes me up and the sun hits my eyes, I realize that it is only in my dreams that this fantasy lies.

All I want to be is a **superhero**, but **superheroes** have powers way beyond me. I think about their powers and what they include. I look in the mirror and think, *I wonder if I can be a* **superhero**.

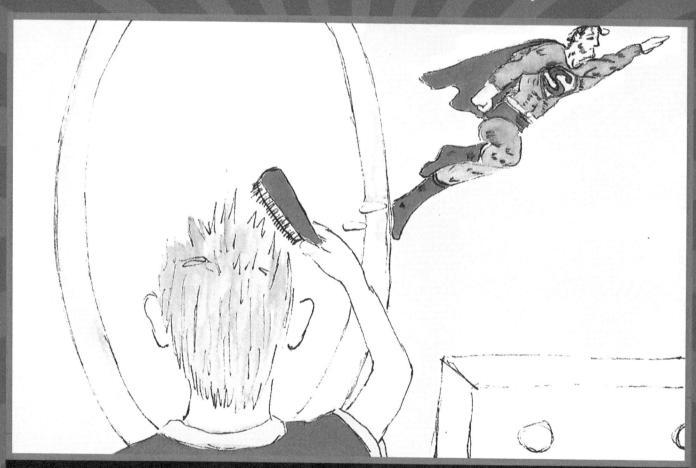

Time for breakfast! A rainbow of healthy foods cover
my plate, fuel for my body, I cannot wait.

After breakfast, I put down the phone and go out for a ride on my red bike, painted with silver racing stripes. The sun shines, and I ride as fast as I can, pretending I am off to save the day once again.

At the playground, I run around with my friend Will, deep in our world of Gotham City. Will is Robin, and I am Batman.

As we are playing, I see the new girl at school on the ground;

she has fallen and scraped her knee.

I help her up, and she says she is OK and that her name is Jenny.

I ask her to join our game; she smiles, and I say, "Let's go! The Joker will get you, Catwoman, if you stay that way." We jump back into our world of finding the villain—Batman, Robin, and Catwoman off to save the day.

I practice baseball with my team, and we work side by side.

Win or lose, it doesn't matter; it's when we work together that we are really a team.

At night I lie on the grass, gazing up at the stars with light so bright they are perfect for a **superhero**. I wish again that I could be one. I imagine the cape that I would wear as I soar through the stars way up there.

I walk into the house, a frown on my face. My mom looks at me as I jump up on her lap. "How can I help turn that frown around?" she asks.

"I want to be a **superhero**, but I am *just me*."

"Just me," she says, a smile on her face. "Let's look at your day and all that you have done. Let's see—how did you start your day again?"

"With food that makes me strong!"

"Didn't you say that your new friend Jenny fell at school and you helped her up?"

"Yes, I did! I helped her when she needed me."

I look up and see Dad and Grandma in the doorway looking
at me. Dad says, "After school, what did you do?"

"You were there, Dad. I practiced baseball with my team," I answer.

He says, "You did, and do you know any superheroes
who team up and work together?"

"Oh, yes! There are the Avengers, and Batman and Robin,
and even the X—Men work with their friends."

Grandma, who has been quiet up until now, says, "So if I understand you right, you are eating foods that make you healthy and strong, getting exercise, and spending time in the sun. I believe these are all things superheroes do. Not only that, but you were kind and helped someone who was in need. What does Superman do when Jimmy Olsen needs him?"

"Oh! He helps him!" I say, surprised to realize that Grandma knows who Jimmy is.

I thought, *Mom, Dad, and Grandma are right. I may not be able to leap over a building or run at super speeds, but I can be a* **superhero** *in my own way.*

I can be strong and kind, and I can work with a team. There are things I am good at!

And as I go to bed, I began to create a new dream in my head. As I drift off into my new world, I imagine all the ways I AM a **superhero**.

In the morning, I wake up with a smile on my face as I remember my dreams. I know that there are things that make me like a **superhero** in my own way.

What ways can you be like a **superhero**?

Remember: you are special and one-of-a-kind and here for a reason!

CPSIA information can be obtained
at www.ICGtesting.com
Printed in the USA
LVHW011252241220
674970LV00004B/128

9 781982 257521